Who Will Be My Pet?

By Stan Tusan
Illustrated by Roy McKie

To Barbara, Cary, and Alison—S.T.

A GOLDEN BOOK • NEW YORK

Western Publishing Company, Inc., Racine, Wisconsin 53404

I had a dog

who ran away.

So I bought a bird

who flew away.
Oh, well.

Then I got some goldfish

who swam away.

So I snared a snake

who slithered away.
Oh, well.

Next I picked a hamster

HAMSTER
SALE

who scampered
away.

So I chose a baby
alligator

who snip-snapped away.
Oh, well.

I was given a rabbit

who hip-hopped away.

So I took a kitten

who tiptoed away.
Oh, well.

Then I met a monkey

who swung away.

So I found a pig

who waddled away.
Oh, well.

Next I roped a cow

who moooved away.

So I sent for a koala

who climbed away.
Oh, well.

Finally I won an elephant

who clumped away.

Suddenly, there was a loud knock at my door.

So I opened it,
and guess who was there!

The dog, the bird,
the goldfish,
the snake, the hamster,
the alligator,

the rabbit, the kitten,
the monkey,
the pig, the cow, the koala,
and the elephant, too.

Oh, well…